The Mother Who Couldn't Describe a Thing if She Could

Shareen K. Murayama

Harbor Editions
Small Harbor Publishing

Cover art: Megan Merchant, "Poeming"
Cover design: Brianna Chapman
Interior design: Ellie Davis
Small Harbor Publishing Managing Editor: Kristiane K. Weeks-Rogers
Small Harbor Publishing Director: Allison Blevins

THE MOTHER WHO COULDN'T DESCRIBE A THING IF SHE COULD
SHAREEN K. MURAYAMA
ISBN 978-1-957248-25-7
Harbor Editions,
an imprint of Small Harbor Publishing

for Randi-Gurl

The Mother Who Couldn't Describe a Thing if She Could

Contents

The Mother Who Couldn't Describe a Thing if She Could

after Mary Ruefle

> *There are five types of mothers. It's true. I read about it the other day during lunch, which is a period of time away from work reserved for bodily functions, like eating or reading. An article is a set of words you usually read by yourself, silently. After reading an article, it could bring you enlightenment or entertainment. Another type of silent words is a confession. I am most like four of the five types of mothers.*

In the Magical Kingdom Called The Suburbs

The individual families decide how many to procreate. The offspring are schooled with books, sports, and hobbies. The individual families become couples in a house with half-filled rooms, holding just-in-case beds for their offsprings. The individual couples work, sleep, retire, and age. They forget having fender benders, how clean a hip breaks. They never see offspring enough. The individual couples worry about the falling action: they treat cancer, install a commode. The ending is always the same: the individual is the last half of the couple. Some offspring return. Some offspring cannot—living in their own magical kingdom called The Suburbs.

Arrhythmia

Imagine a line between the nipples. Put your hands on the center of the chest right below that line. No, you don't have to remove the bra. This is the scene I imagine will break my Adam. Splayed out on the promenade, I heed to their heel, covered by other demands, to stop real pain: when life outlives your life-long partner.

Internally, I forget to count the dark: your last birthday, the two-hand count before retiring. Meanwhile, I'm crumpling a tinge of blue, like showcase lights in front of Nordstrom's Rack, worrying about oxygen. How can you want what you can no longer see?

I'm lying to myself on the sidewalk of passersby and wedding anniversaries, thinking jellyfish have no brains and no hearts. Some of us are spared questioning what's fueling through our limbs. Some of us drift and settle for the ocean floor.

When my dad was in the care home, he needed help with his advance health directives. *Would you want CPR or other resuscitation if your heart were to stop beating?* It's an uncontrollable sound, like crying, that rises and falls with each birthday and holiday card. Each song floods the banks and rivers. *Do you want to donate your eyes?*

After my father's and husband's deaths, I wintered on writing; I panted through pain. When my waters broke, they husband-stitched my fingertips after pushing out what couldn't be said: thirty compressions and a few rescue breaths, my body spoons over a reef. How can you see what doesn't belong to you anymore?

I think my heart may have turned on me with little fists, when my dad agreed to resuscitation and said, *Try. At least one time.*

Deficiency

I have a hard time imagining four pairs of ample feet draping out beneath a blanket's edge. My grandfather was the oldest of twelve; my mother, of eight. Both were reared under one roof, in a rural town on something like a farm, selling something like string beans. Maybe the children ate in shifts or fielded for themselves.

Perhaps running out of space unleashed the children to moor beneath dusk's umbrella, a water hose, a handful of food, and relish in a voided second.

Under our quaint roof, the side dishes tend to loiter, squatting on our bistro table: ramekins of kimchi, sliced fruits, takuan, a chawan bowl of black beans with cilantro salad. And then, two dinner plates.

Nothing can be spaced out.

It reflects both my atomically privileged lifestyle as well as my challenges as an underachieved renter. Some call my sanctuary on the mountain, wasted space: where the not-quite-successful grownups have our backs up against by-now-they-shoulda and just don't talk about it. The varying straights and turns consumed less of the distance than I had expected in the expanse of living while trying to earn a life.

As a writer, this draws me to wonder about spaces in letters and sighs. The unoccupied portions in numbers and negatives—especially now with so many at the onset of revisiting the workspace. We are preparing to go back in time to a dimension we believed to be dogmatic. There's so much allowance for what's not provided. Everything's so complex: the area needed for perfection, the distance between a wink.

I often think about my mother's last years and how sundowning is also filled with too many holes. The square-footage of her five-bedroom house was filled with less feet. And how symptoms like disoriented and incoherent contained a lot of *oh that's terrible* sounds. As she grew fragile, she occupied less and less of herself. Space became the area around everything that existed: her billowing blouse, the unsteady floor, a phonebook she forgot how to open.

Even now, as I kern these lines, I worry about spacing, the seductive errors in reading between them. I'm saying I care and I don't care if I never become a homeowner. I'm grateful and ashamed that I haven't always sprouted fruits. If negative space is a necessary boundary to define something, like a town or trust, I wonder which congenital spaces I'm afraid to sound out?

Both of my parents were very inactive; their thoracic cavities called for interventions. More was taken than restored. If space allows us to make sense of how things move from and on, then sitting on my kitchen stool with the evening winds beyond my touch, I'm content with my wonderings and being (somewhat) brave to acknowledge the spaces under this roof and anticipate the weight of tomorrow night's twinkling.

Because a Mission Statement is What I'm Supposed to be Doing

My ignorance about music is like the ugly parts of me, one hand strums the recognizable parts of my body. My mouth opens and I want to be here, but how does the bass keep us in rhythm among the grass cutters? I tap my Air Force Ones to the city's noise—I know that you know I'm off my body. If I could live ten times bolder, I wouldn't have to fake the two-step. I'll pick my theme song for my next life. We sing-song *knot.bunny-ears.wrap.* when teaching toddlers about security; we wrestle doubt, anchor non-skid socks on loved ones and dementia. Why haven't we learned how not to fall? One day I'll love you; I'll press my cheek against the cold kitchen tile. How does one stand the injustices in the world? That's a type of love, too, isn't it? Start with what you want to say. A family freezes or is crossed by a river crossing. Keep it simple: People are dying to get in. People are dying to get ahead of next month's paycheck. Keep it conversational: If we could save just a little or ourselves. If I were ten times bolder, the syllables would fit the melody.

I am guilty of being a me-first and perfectionist type of mother. I've a history of being an unpredictable mom who tries to come off as a best friend because I don't know how to set healthy boundaries. A boundary is a protected space that is not a kill zone or deadline. What an ocean is to an island. Like a daughter. Both island and daughter are nouns. Both are birthed in liquid, and over time, their exterior hardens.

Fig and Yield

Irony is confessing I often blank on the word *idiom* even though I associate it with the word *idiot*. When the whole is not deducible by its parts, how is a life well-lived? Which traditions should be dog-eared or rubbed out?

I belong to an indigenous group that refuses to be recognized by their ruling power.

On our island, we ring in the new year twice: December 31st and Lunar New Year. We love our traditions, and this week the news will be lined with two kinds of stories: firework-related injuries and Fukubukuro. The latter being culturally appropriated from Japanese culture meaning Lucky Bag Sales from various merchants.

I also belong to that ruling power.

The headlines are peppered with body parts: A 7-year-old girl in Kailua suffered a hand injury; an 11-year-old boy, an eye injury; a woman, her hand, and other parts of her body. Sadly, on Kauai, a 34-year-old man died while trying to light *a firework that malfunctioned*, meaning *failed to function normally*; meaning careless or murder.

It's frustrating defending one's existence.

Fireworks and celebrations. These things go: hand and hand and other parts. They say noise and fire keep evil spirits away, making space for good luck to flock in. Maybe our traditions are superstitious. Some of us believe spending a thousand to four thousand dollars on aerials will afford us a bigger return. Like Fukubukuro.

One of my cultural identities has also bombed the country, the island, I was born on.

When purchasing a mystery bag, one expects to receive twice the value of items nobody wanted in the first place. Everyone's on the bandwagon: Tori Richard, Tory Burch, Local Motion, Michael Kors. Many wake early on holiday to be first in line to gamble. Is it risk, consideration, or coveting the prize, as in a thing given for outstanding achievement or meaning *absolute* and *totally*, as in *a prized idiot?*

One of my ethnic identities has savagely killed, humiliated, and violated many indigenous groups.

I discovered that 98 percent of fireworks purchased by Americans are hand made in China. I wonder if this unit of time, a Gregorian calendar pinning seasons to dates that will fig and yield, is a calculated ceremony, as in something that's evolved, its meaning changed over time.

I currently reside on an island that I bombed, that I stole, that I profited from a country's invasion.

In a Tultepec warehouse, just north of Mexico City, twenty-four people were killed, forty-nine injured.

I'm not sure how the words *fireworks, explosions, common* reside in one sentence, where *sentence* means *punishment actually ordered.* To show one's hand means to reveal one's intention, like plumes of smoke rising in the distance.

Historically, I am the colonizer and the colonized; violator and infiltrated; but mostly, I carry the weight of shame.

It's a container, pasted paper, and string—how aerial fireworks are made. But it's the fuse that allows for a time delay, so it explodes at the appropriate altitude.

Vision Test

Standing twenty feet away, can you read the bottom line: did you live your life right? Which view is better, one or two? A scattering or an eco-friendly burial? Your eyes or your skin? Maybe you wish to hold on to them.

I often invited my children to spend time with my grandmother. Later, when they became adults, they conceded how unusual it was to fan out beach towels and deal out bentos on the graveyard's manicured lawn. Presbyopia, a natural part of aging, is the gradual loss of your eyes' ability to focus on nearby objects.

One or two? The number of medical opinions sought, even though the diagnosis is the same. She has no partner or children, so you learn how to bathe and wash your best friend's hair. Her myopathy disables all fingers; her left foot hooks over the tub. You worry like the weighted balance of a spoon. How is one to bear down, twist and turn when living with cancer?

My mother had gifted all her daughters jade pieces: sap green bangles and lavender drop earrings. A childproof piece I don everyday: a jade pendant heart, my talisman. It's opaque and translucent, green veins swirl, a cord around my neck. In the end, both my mom and best friend didn't recognize me.

One or two? Acceptance or hope? Grab any metal object, a knife or a needle. Scratch the surface just so. You're hoping not to see signs of permanent damage. Jade is supposed to be the protector of generations, living and deceased. It's the jewel of heaven. A heart of stone.

Blue Space

My heart and my house are shrinking at a phenomenal rate. Parts of you
—your eyeglasses, pack of cigs, flannel, and lube—were assembled on
my nightstand. The doctors have no diagnosis about doors that won't
budge, cedar-like floors lit yellow by nightlight. It used to sadden you to
know I've a history of bumping into dark things.

As for the shriveling of my heart, the doctors monitor it: weakly, a chair
leg scratches the floor in an auditorium. The doctors claim the heart will
chafe; the body will attempt to reabsorb its mistakes. My grandfather
showed me love once; he placed a praying mantis against my childhood.
Men have always corded me to wild things. A buckskin horse is a
testament when it leans into another one of its kind.

Maybe I'm mixing my metaphors. I'm trying to say, sometimes loving
oneself is not reciprocal. I can touch but never hold myself. Even if I
choose love, the end product will always be one.

"Will it hurt?" I ask the doctors. Believing that the sky was real, a bird
pings against glass. I pity its reaching for vegetation, an idyllic landscape.
I shield the body from predators with a colander and wait for the shock
to subside.

A marriage means more than one thing. Marriage has a beginning and end. A marriage can make people happy or sad. A daughter could be born within or without that season. When a marriage ends, sometimes the daughter carries on even though she may feel like an island.

Mother Warns Us of Men

Like the sun, Father disappears every day after work, after drinking too much awamori. He hurricanes other spirits with spirits. He once twisted the necks of two half-eyed kittens, so leafy their bones—but what do we know of love, of fish thrashing on shore? I, too, am afraid to wake up in foreign spaces.

To save our necks, Mother teaches us to walk with our whole face down. My sisters and I forget that we carry the same ears. We are waiting, like fishing poles, for something to move us. Mother calls it saving face. *Will it hurt*, we ask, imagining our heads paraded for other families to approve, to wed. We are waiting to use our faces.

When Yuta comes over, she armors father's body with songs of victory. Warrior or demon, we are not sure which one is Father, so in our dreams we offer him our faces as shields, even though they are meaty, like the underside of peaches. Father dislikes peaches. In our dreams, Father loses our love; he loses his face. Every fall, we pool the fallen leaves, dried like kittens. We raise our heads and jump into battle.

When Father comes home through the sickness, Mother greets him with her whole face down.

The Departure

After my daughter and I left Open City, I'd already missed Cuban coffees, the lions or zebra crackers that fluttered on saucer edges. Without defining lines, it's hard to diagnose the shape of your animal. My taxi dropped her off, while I was Dulles-bound.

Bungalow homes with slanted roofs, counterclockwise past the elm and oak. Too often we're directed to pan out as one of us grows smaller—a hint of snow freckled on a chest scan—How does a mother prepare to leave her daughter's side?

The driver lobs his two-cents backwards—"You two close, like sisters?"

I recall being home in winter swells after a wipeout, my body is pinned under while arms and legs are ragdolled. It's against our nature not to panic no matter the burning in one's chest. She's three at the hospital, bottom lip stitched sans asphalt; when she's older, the nurse draws the delivery door; already, I am on the other side.

The sun sets like dried leather, and I say, "Yes, very much—like mother and daughter."

More than an Acquired Taste

"You distinguish yourself by not doing what others do."
—Alan Dundes, American Folklorist

My cousins and I pinch our noses, squealing from the absent parts of the pig not on Baabaa's cutting board. Whenever she cooks pig's feet soup, we dare one another to lick its cold skin, supple like a rubber eraser. Having touched its elongated toes before, we'd grown up indifferent as Adam to an array of offal; what we knew of God's touch, we experienced through Baabaa's beatings.

Our classmates squeal at us, *Filthy animals!* We gnaw on toes enveloped in their own shit. When we asked Baabaa if this was true, she said, *Who don't eat cheat time from time?* Only our eyes laugh when she says *cheat* instead of *shit*. We don't correct her, especially after the first time Jiji went missing, returning home a week later. He was so drunk, Baabaa had to undress and bathe her husband. He reeked of beer and piss—*Cheat!*—and something sweet she'd encountered before. *Cheat! Cheat! Cheat!*

It's dizzying, having necessary parts lopped off. Baabaa never speaks of her family in Okinawa, the first island she lived on. She speaks Japanese and Okinawan, but to us, she barks lifted words until we nod pretending we understand English. The second time Jiji disappeared, Baabaa beat him over the head when he came home, threatened to slice off his boto next time. About the bullies, Baabaa tells us, *Mo bettah they scare you away, than say they want some, too.*

Beneath the pig's chalky skin, tiny red vessels bloom, reminding us of the blue veins on Mary Jane's white cheeks, the one classmate who doesn't tease us. She says, *The Filipinos eat dog; the Hawaiians ate Captain Cook.* I want to believe she's my friend, so I steal a mechanical pencil from her fancy pencil box, a magnetic clasp secures its contents. We don't buy what we can't afford for all the cousins, so we carry our pencils like switchblades, safeguarding our place in the world.

At school, half of our teachers are White, the other half are Asian, but it doesn't matter since our family's partial to famous movie stars. My eldest cousins Grace (Kelly) and Sandra (Dee), look alike and trade places to confuse their White teachers. We have five uncles Bob (Hope), three uncles Dean (Martin); and four uncles George (Burns). Baabaa believes wearing English names would make us more American. Except when Jiji falls asleep in front of the tv, and the national anthem plays, we feel less patriotic as the flag stutters up the pole like a ghost watching its own back, aiming for a hole in the sky to return to the other side.

By the late afternoon, everything falls off the bone. Caught in Baabaa's rolling boil, the aunties are shooed out of the kitchen. She adds

23

half-moons of daikon, knotted konbu strips, mustard cabbage, bamboo shoots, and handfuls of Chinese parsley.

We discard inedible bits in a bowl at the center of the children's table. The younger ones watch as we build a tower of bones. Founded on masticated leftovers, this is how we build a family. The youngest ones follow our fingers, our faces, back to our fingers. No one talks as beads of fat the color of second-hand pearls nestle between our knuckles. We slurp gel and joints, insert fingers to peel back the fatty skin, like wrapping paper, like a gift we can never replace.

When an island appears attached to the main landform, it's called tambolo, meaning cushion or pillow. My daughter wore jeans under a dress once, I ordered her to change her clothes. Did she want people to laugh at her, meaning me, the me-first mother? Other names are barrier or spit. The main thing to remember is that the attachment is mostly invisible.

Maximum Allowance

She used to be adept at becoming invisible. To help matters, she saved her words for essential desires. Ten words a week was a gentle reminder to her parents that they still owned a child. She materialized to expend two words—roller skates—as she pointed to her birthday on the calendar. It was especially expensive when they forced her to use her words. What do you say to your uncle who brought you this gift? Shoulders shrugged. What do you say?! She sighed. *Thank you very much, for the teddy bear.* Eight. whole. words. She turned her face away from his chest-belly in order to breathe. He bent down lower to brush his coral against her skin, but she refused to spend another word on him.

He flew in every year to visit them. He took pleasure in grabbing and tickling her feet until her body stiffened, inadvertently squeezed warm drops of pee onto her underwear. He knew, then, to stop. For a whole year, she surveyed her uncle as a stranger, captained her foot as gangrenous, endured family as phantom pains one must tolerate until she was desensitized. She smirked when his face froze with disappointment at her non-writhing and non-begging. Another time, he reeled her in by grasping both her hands. I'll show you something, he said. He tugged her index fingers free and propped them together. This is the church. He bent her pinkies together. Lift the tip of the rod skyward. This is the steeple. He laced and unlaced her thumbs. He opened her doors. See all the people? But when she looked inside her malformed hands, her world hung upside down. Do you see all the people who love you? She looked harder, a single-size family, a congregation, dangled from the rafters. She flexed her fingers, igniting their feet to dance.

When the fish slows down, it is time to go to work. Their laughter meant lust, meant surrendering to hands with more power than hers. This is how to build a place of worship, where the foundation of obedience is half open fists. She could not make herself invisible. Do you see it, he asked? It didn't matter if she used her last two words. He could see her. This is the church. This is the steeple.

Thursday Night at Lucky's Liquor Store

When the semi flipped on its side, cows were launched like bowling pins across multiple lanes. Several died inside the truck. Eventually, many uprighted like dice. The driver lay dying, his belly forming pleats on the steering wheel.

After slamming into an ice freezer, a brown-and-white heifer shook its head. Some were caught four miles down the highway, its diminishing lines going somewhere, going nowhere.

The dying driver wished his girlfriend could know the squeeze of his hand. Her stained lips that hung on his bathroom mirror would close the night for him. Maybe if he weren't dying, she'd reconsider his question.

Outside the hooven beats padded nothing like police or ambulance. Just glacial were the fumes inflating the shattered cab. For three days she had ghosted him, through mud-turned fields, snow sugared on windshield— even wipers lied: *Come back, come back.*

Even if she'd occasionally squeaked too much whiskey; never dividing equally his and hers. He was everything she didn't want for the long ride.

Before the trailer tipped over like cows, before the cows burst through the roof like a birthday cake surprise, he remembered how he'd gifted her open stars, piped buttercream around a silver band.

The brown-and-white appeared on the other side of the shattered glass. How he wished they could see the view from his side—muted lights or setting stars, the gauzy snow lacing his eyes shut.

Sometimes a daughter is born on an island and never leaves. Even her own perfectionist mother moved to California for business school, but the daughter declares it on a bucket list. A bucket list is a list of items one challenges themselves to cross off before one dies, the ultimate deadline. A finish line drawn in everyone's future. Some ignore it, some are weighted by its pressing, some are prepared to cross over, to cross out, or to leave unfinished.

Run the Numbers

"It is a joy to be hidden and a disaster not to be found."
—Donald Winnicott

"I had sex with so-so this summer." This was one student's answer when a probationary teacher asked the classist-favored question, "What did you do this summer?" I've stopped asking that question. Lately, I've been counting because statistics say one in three girls (and one in five boys) are sexually abused before their 18th birthday. I find no comfort knowing we have this in common.

One. Chinese American, tall, lanky, glasses: She's a number.

Two. Greek American, fair skinned, dark eyeliner: She is part of a whole, of a bigger number.

Three. Filipino, Japanese, Hawaiian American, bright smile, bangs. I take her and divide by a hundred. I take her and multiply by six seconds. She is taken by five or one. She is multiplied in her prime. I take her place. I would take her place. I would take her place. Place is never zero, never forgotten. No one believes us. One is a prime number.

She is number. I am number.

It was the slicing that always stirred me. Halving the wolf's belly to rebirth Little Red and Grandmother, as if I, too, wanted to absorb another body. The lessons of death are pastoralized via Bambi or Dumbo, but what lessons of sex are gleaned from trial and error? And do these students live in times where errors are amenable?

How horrifying to imagine them as elementary students with permanent teeth growing in, adult canines getting closer. When does/did it happen? Maybe ten, twenty years from now or never, parents might discover they were home when it happened—and it will almost never kill them.

If I lived ten times more boldly, I would want to know if this is the summer when their shells grew numb, when copper wires got crossed between being beautiful and being used.

I do not have a degree in counseling or psychology. I am not a trauma specialist. But I survived trauma, like one-third of my students in my classes. I was sexually abused between the ages of six and ten. It wasn't the violation and early sexual arousal that ruined me, but the lack of voice or character to stand up for my body against "family" members. But what am I saying? I was six.

When an elder says you're bad, you're beautiful, you're sexy, come here, I believe what they tell me. Even today, I identify with all those modifiers. Can't I be a survivor of sex abuse and still love sex? I'm bad at many things, but I think of myself as a good person; I'm beautiful and insecure; I'm sexy and work to maintain a healthy relationship with sex.

If the statistics are accurate for this year's group of students, and next year's, shouldn't there be more conversations? More services and support? Maybe now is/is not the time to ask my female students to write down their words. To tell ourselves of the darkest forest we've crawled through.

Infiltration

Tomorrow they will scrape and sell the last salt blocks, crusted on the volcanic crater called Aliapaʻakai. Sandwiched between sun and Pacific, the salt will be shipped abroad. No one on Oʻahu will smell the burning resin of trees, the briny smoke trailing from incense sticks.

> But today two sisters celebrate a new homecoming. They carry salt, red dirt, and a bird from Kauaʻi. Or they drop the items and scallop two craters: Aliamanu (salt-encrusted bird) and Aliapaʻakai (salt-encrusted lake). Two homes for two goddesses.

Tomorrow, the Salt Lake community will learn that a town hall was held, approved by a majority. The lake will be sold and filled with a golf course, a country club.

> But today, we celebrate the new high school opening up. We race our bikes along the lake's snaked edges. We are invisible like the wind that scores lines on the lake, reminding me of my grandmother's wrinkles.

Tomorrow, 27,000 gallons of fuel will leak from the U.S. Navy's tanks below Red Hill, which is adjacent to the now-filled Salt Lake. Nothing will be done to rectify or prevent it from happening again.

> But today we believe someone is looking out for us. Someone is doing the work for us as we reuse utensils, plate our tongues with inclusivity. We worry for our aging kupuna, while the dying live on a different schedule than the working.

Tomorrow, Oʻahu's main aquifer will be contaminated, a hundred feet below Red Hill. Over 400,000 residents, from Halawa to Maunalua, will receive an emergency text alert:

> WATER QUALITY EMERGENCY FOR THIS AREA.
> All Oʻahu residents with medical conditions and children under age six should refrain from drinking tap water from their homes until further notice.

But today, we hold our breath over water. We close our eyes, hold out for a different ending.

53 Minutes

Like a bronze-colored sky god, he extends his arms to his sides. He bows his head in service to her expansive beauty. He turns to grab his board, but before entering the surf, he marks the sand with his feet—maybe in x's. He repeats this motion three times as if he's wiping his feet clean before entering someone's house.

Yesterday, I listened to her breathe. She called me from her bed in hospice. She breathes a heavy *hello* as if questioning why I called her. I know she's confused. So am I. "You want me to just talk to you? So you know someone's here with you?"

Some rituals are born from the desire to keep us safe. Some pancake on the sand to round out their spines. Some lift their children toward the ephemeral blue; wrestle a bad relationship, up and over. Maintain annual check ups. Celebrate a life.

My ritual begins at the start of the path. In my head, I chant, *Akua, please keep everyone safe from injury and harm. Keep everyone safe from injury and harm.* I repeat this at least three times, until I turn the cliff and see the white wash, two-three feet high, and know it's going to be frothy out there. Sometimes the ocean is a safe place to land.

I know this is the start of the end. I tell her it's storming on top of my mountain. "The birds have gone quiet for now." I can't bring myself to hang up, so I wait for my phone to die.

I say *injury and harm* knowing they are two different things. Even though both could be inflicted by self and others, harm lingers—whether in spirit or body, whether temporary or permanent.

Relocation is when someone changes their geographic position for a period of time. The individual takes their belongings to a place they want to belong. New names hang on different streets, but destinations remain the same: work, home, ground and sky. The unpredictable mother dreams of relocating, but I think she knows only the scenery changes. Generally, the person generally remains the same.

For Richer

For our next anniversary, we'll commit to adding that fourth kitchen we always talked about. I'll encourage you to approve the plans for the 12-stall garage, your 16-story man cave. We'll laugh when we resort to cell phones to locate each other when we're home.

Every week on special occasions, we'll exchange gifts: a butterfly house with pink bow, enough bass to fill a 15-acre lake. We'll have his and her private islands. At the end of the night, traveling back to our bedroom could be too pedestrian, so you'll stay there, and I'll stay here. We'll laugh when we resort to our cell phones to kiss each other goodnight.

One day, you'll trek me through your 32-story man-cave. You'll admit how mainstream you feel about darkness, so you'll knock down a wall, create an open-faced city. How you used to like your eggs.

I'll be impressed with your new life, jealous of new friends in corner bars you've had built, the waitress who flirts with you, who needed someplace to stay, just her and her kid. A few years later, you'll add a preschool, no time for vacations. We used to love skiing indoors, remember?

We'll sigh and remember what it was like before—rotating on our sides in the double bed with one zip code, the warmth of your hand on my thigh, a pedestal sink with no room for toothbrushes. We'd cop a feel as we untangled legs. We'd do our what if's, our maybe's, someday's, synchronized, easy over—how I used to like my eggs.

Even if I'm not the Golden Child

For Asian identifiers who are often described as being "so nice"

1. I've almost completed my atude of "auntie" Marilyn Chin who exudes badass-fierce energy. She says, *ALL you bitches is my son!*

   SQUEE! I jaw drop wonder if I was even–ever born
   under a sign with too much water with hands above my head
   upright, like citizens or animals with questions.

2. Let me raise my winged
                     my broken   waiting for self-permission.

3. I'm supposed to be _____, but I'm only gracious—polite —a dinner plate before being plated. I channel ancestors pitched on a mountain, arms robed forward, like Charlton Heston as Moses. I channel Charlton Heston as Moses not at all disconcerted about his Asian niece. He tries on some Japanese conversation—like tying knots on leather sandals—I don't speak Japanese.

4. I channel ancestral animals and guides. I've never been good at church so I meditate the Geico Gecko. I confess I don't know how not to be nice. The Geico Gecko palm faces himself with somewhat appendages.

5. I'm still having problems with my Purchase Order screen. It still doesn't show my past orders. My daughter says to just stop, that Facebook posts are not Customer Service.

6. The Latin root for vulture is "vultur" meaning "to pluck or tear." The entry beneath lists vulva, from Latin vulva, meaning "to turn or twist."

   SQUEE! I jaw drop wonder if I was even—ever bad sexy,
   powerful. Moses and the gecko are silent. I channel Godzilla
   instead.

7. Perhaps I'm doomed to always be nice. I think I'll go back to my atude of "auntie" Marilyn Chin who exudes bad-ass-fierce energy. She says, *ALL you bitches is my son!*

Before Rapid Eye Movement

At night, I needle words into a song. I edit myself with eyes drawn shut between worlds as most of my wants are on the other side. At night, I discuss things calmly with my mother. I'm not sure if this is something she wants or needs. I'm not sure if the not-living have needs.

The most ordinary days are to be feared the most. I know you slept on Monday, did or did not greet Tuesday. I found you on a Wednesday. When the medical examiner left a message, I forgot to return their call. Surely you can see why I refuse to dream.

When my body temperature drops and my heart rate slows, I torture myself envisioning the death of my loved ones: a cannonball and windshield, a concrete egress on the thirtieth floor. Onset labor flashes and my water breaks. In each scenario, I appear on scene too late. In my dreams, there will be bottles and pills and star-gazing. I am reluctant to attach to new people.

At night, I am confused by my loneliness and its warm company.

Word of Mouth

"You are whatever room you're in."
—a Japanese proverb

I want to place my hand over my heart and vow I'm still human at least
that's what the morning headline offers for suffering for loss I've a great
imagination but today I'll inspect my gear tongue and teeth operate in
present tense but maybe today maybe I'll attempt to want future tense
which billows toward desire   it's illegal

to buy only one guinea pig in Switzerland I texted to see if you missed
me because herd animals need at least one other and single cats should
be able to see other single cats parrots goldfish and I are content in the
first room we enter generally I answer to any name you call me what is
loved can be wedged in a single wide sentence   on screen

it never says THE END because we're supposed to already know I am
born a boat slips through channels what does it mean to play dead pasted
center on a rock is a sea star one arm elbows over sleeping on itself its
tubed feet like fallen trees rows of stubbed teeth I practice lip reading I
study menus rehearse being asked what do you want   in life

you taught me the three bite rule the first whispers hello the last reserved
for the irreversible   sometimes if you're lucky you get the one with the
most spackling which is rare I get the un-rare ones maybe I shouldn't lie
it's not like I believe in that kind of cause and effect relationship
sometimes I unswirl   over semantics

evergreen ever succulent our b roll is the girth of our goat I love us more
when we say the best lines at the same time I might be afraid to ask for
help I can't find words just in case words or in other words stay with me
crazy cord

and wire birds of the atoll words of tomorrow's cattle music

Fails to Understand Requirements

We were warned never to clip our nails at night. There's a desperate spirit who'll curse us beyond our grandmother's waking one morning, her black hair gone all white at the parting of her teen-aged son.

Our teacher carved question marks at our beginning, said we'd fail if we can't distinguish between stories and myths.

We argued: Loss is also a hook that drags us along.

An arrow targeted our grandmother's fading is a sign that we overestimated our audience's ability to connect.

Being non-respondent for a year is also a conflict—a struggle between two forces. We also labeled it as a type of resolution.

After returning from her travels, we asked our grandmother if she'd brought us anything: a handwritten note, a nub of a tooth, his black comb that we couldn't use.

In our story, Uncle plays the dynamic character. Our teacher double-underlined his name, *But he's DEAD!*

Red comments in the margins in a sign that we underestimated our audience's intelligence.

She untied what she held, dividing a lock of his hair among us cousins, which we pressed between pages for another story to be read, underscored.

The Complete Mother combines the best elements of all types of mothers. Complete can mean balanced or finalized. I am guilty of being a me-first and perfectionist type of mother. I've a history of being an unpredictable mom who tries to come off as a best friend. I am most like four of the five types of mothers. Shouldn't there be more types of mothers?

Acknowledgements
in Order of Appearance

Title of Collection (after Mary Ruefle's "The Woman Who Couldn't Describe a Thing if She Could," Paris Review, 2016)

Deficiency. ((mac)ro(mic), 2020)

Arrhythmia (MORIA, Winner Best Microfictions, 2021)

In the Magical Kingdom Called The Suburbs (Flash Boulevard, 2021)

*Fig and Yield (CRAFT CNF Contest 2020 Honorable Mention, Finalist Ray Ventre Nonfiction Prize, 2021)

Vision Test (Revolutionary Review, 2022)

Blue Space (Porter House Review, 2022)

Mother Warns Us of Men (Smokelong Quarterly, 2022)

More than an Acquired Taste (Flash Frog Fiction, 2022)

*Maximum Allowance (CRAFT CNF Contest 2021 Honorable Mention, 2022)

Thursday Night at Lucky's Liquor Store (WINNER Fractured Lit. Anthology Prize, 2021)

Run the Numbers (The Palisades Review, 2023)

Infiltration (Goat's Milk Mag, 2021)

53 Minutes (Scrawl Place, 2021)

For Richer (Wigleaf, 2023)

Even if I'm not the Golden Child (The McNeese Review, 2022)

Fails to Understand Requirements (Practicing Anthropology, 2023)

*Titles publicly recognized, not published

Shareen K. Murayama is the author of two poetry books *Housebreak* (Bad Betty Press, 2022) and *Hey Girl, Are You in the Experimental Group* (Harbor Editions, 2022). She's a Japanese American, Okinawan American poet and educator, a Jack Hazard Fellow, Pushcart Prize nominee, as well as Best Small Fictions & Best of the Net nominee. Featured in *Poets & Writers Debut 5 Over 50 Authors*, she lives in Honolulu and supports the #litcommunity @AmBusyPoeming.

About Small Harbor Publishing

Small Harbor Publishing is a 501c3 nonprofit organization. Our goal is to publish unique and diverse voices. We are a feminist press, and we are committed to diversity and inclusion. We strive to bring new voices to a devoted and expanding readership.

Small Harbor Publishing began in 2018 with the first issue of *Harbor Review*. The magazine is an online space where poetry and art converse. *Harbor Review* quickly grew and now publishes reviews and runs multiple micro chapbook competitions, including the Washburn Prize and the Editor's Prize.

In July 2020, Small Harbor Publishing was officially incorporated and began Harbor Editions. Harbor Editions accepts submissions through a chapbook open reading period, a hybrid chapbook open reading period, the Marginalia Series, and the Laureate Prize.

In 2023, Harbor Anthologies began with a mission to promote texts that explore social justice issues and highlight marginalized writers.

If you would like to support Small Harbor Publishing, please visit our "About" page at smallharborpublishing.com/about.

Made in the USA
Middletown, DE
29 August 2024

59903280R00028